Learning to Read, Step by Step!

Ready to Read   Preschool–Kindergarten
• big type and easy words • rhyme and rhythm • picture clues
For children who know the alphabet and are eager to
begin reading.

Reading with Help   Preschool–Grade 1
• basic vocabulary • short sentences • simple stories
For children who recognize familiar words and sound out
new words with help.

Reading on Your Own   Grades 1–3
• engaging characters • easy-to-follow plots • popular topics
For children who are ready to read on their own.

Reading Paragraphs   Grades 2–3
• challenging vocabulary • short paragraphs • exciting stories
For newly independent readers who read simple sentences
with confidence.

Ready for Chapters   Grades 2–4
• chapters • longer paragraphs • full-color art
For children who want to take the plunge into chapter books
but still like colorful pictures.

STEP INTO READING® is designed to give every child a successful
reading experience. The grade levels are only guides; children will progress
through the steps at their own speed, developing confidence in their reading.
The F&P Text Level on the back cover serves as another tool to help you
choose the right book for your child.

Remember, a lifetime love of reading starts with a single step!

Visit us on the Web!
StepIntoReading.com
randomhouse.com/kids
BerenstainBears.com

Educators and librarians, for a variety of teaching tools, visit us at
RHTeachersLibrarians.com

Library of Congress Cataloging-in-Publication Data
Berenstain, Stan.
Bears on wheels / by Stan and Jan Berenstain.
  pages cm. — (Step into reading. Step 1)
"Originally published in a different form by Random House Children's Books, New York, in 1969."
Summary: An acrobatic act begins with one bear on a unicycle and ends with twenty-one bears
and sixteen wheels flying through the air.
ISBN 978-0-385-39136-8 (pbk.) — ISBN 978-0-375-97362-8 (lib. bdg.) —
ISBN 978-0-385-39137-5 (ebook)
[1. Acrobatics—Fiction. 2. Bears—Fiction. 3. Counting.] I. Berenstain, Jan. II. Title.
PZ7.B4483Bc 2014 [E]—dc23 2013046655

Printed in the United States of America
10 9 8 7 6 5 4 3 2 1

This book has been officially leveled by using the F&P Text Level Gradient™ Leveling System.

The Berenstain Bears®
BEARS ON WHEELS

Stan & Jan Berenstain

Random House 🏠 New York

One bear.

One wheel.

One bear on one wheel.

Two bears on one wheel.

Three on one.

Four on one.

Four bears on one wheel.

One bear on two wheels.

Four on two.

One on one again.

One on one.

Three on three.

None on four.

Four on none.

One on one again.

Five on one.

Five bears on one.

Five bears on none.

Ten on one.

One bear on five wheels.

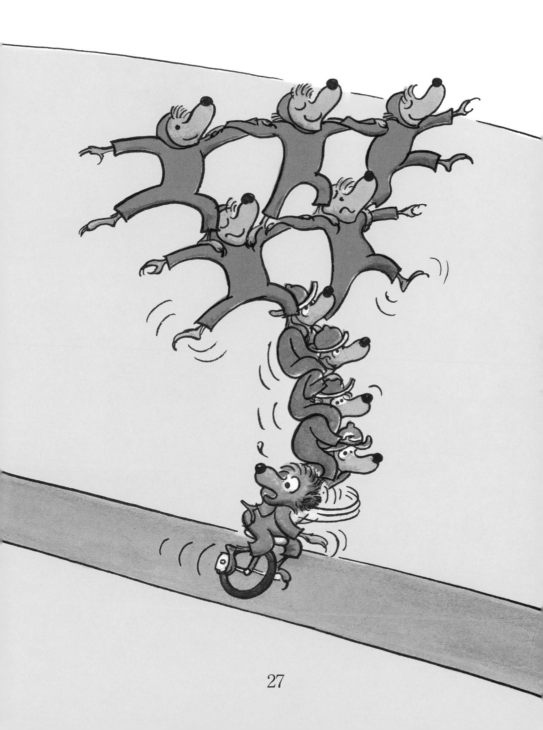

One on five.

Ten on one.

Ten on ten.

Twenty-one on none.

One on one again.